Walt Disney Pictures

THE Return To OZ STORYBOOK

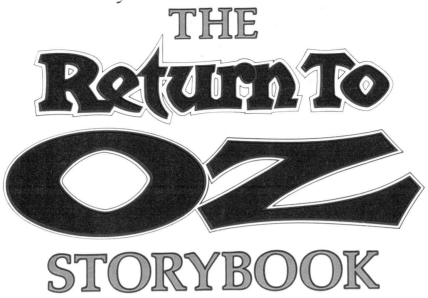

Based on the motion picture from Walt Disney Pictures
Executive Producer Gary Kurtz
Produced by Paul Maslansky
Screenplay by Walter Murch & Gill Dennis
Directed by Walter Murch

A GOLDEN BOOK · NEW YORK
Western Publishing Company, Inc., Racine, Wisconsin 53404

"What can I do to make you happy?" said Dr. Worley.

He smiled and Dorothy looked away. The smile scared her.

"Your aunt says you've been waking up at night," said the doctor. "Why?"

"I think about my friends," said Dorothy. "They need me and they want me to come back to Oz."

Dorothy then told how the tornado had howled across the fields six months ago, and how it had picked up Uncle Henry's farmhouse with Dorothy in it. It had whirled the house to a wonderful place called Oz. In Oz Dorothy had met the Tin Woodman and the Cowardly Lion and the very clever Scarecrow, and she had visited the bejeweled Emerald City.

"The Scarecrow is the King of Oz now," she said. "He needs me. They all need me. I want to go to them, but Aunt Em says there's no such place as Oz."

Dr. Worley continued to smile. "If you were to go to Oz," said he, "how would you get there?"

"I'm not sure, but I know there's a way," Dorothy said. "It has something to do with this."

She took a key out of her pocket. "I saw it fall from the sky last night. I thought it was a meteor, but this morning Billina found it. It's from Oz. You can see the letters 'O' and 'Z' in the thumbpiece."

The doctor took the key and looked at it. He handed it back. "And who is Billina?" he asked.

"My pet chicken."

"I see. And when you were in Oz, how did you get home to Kansas again?"

"With my ruby slippers," said Dorothy. "I put them on and wished myself home, only... only I lost the slippers. They fell off on the way back."

Aunt Em had been sitting silent, listening, while all this went on. Now the doctor turned to her. "I know just the thing to cheer Dorothy up," he said.

He went to a closet and opened a door. Dorothy saw a thing that looked like a grandfather's clock. It wasn't a clock, however. Instead of numbers it had dials and switches that resembled eyes and a mouth.

"This will take away the bad dreams," said the doctor.

Dorothy saw something move. She turned. There was a little girl with blond hair in the doorway.

Dr. Worley did not notice the little girl. He was talking to Aunt Em. Dorothy must stay at his clinic for a week, he said. Then she would be completely well again.

The little girl slipped away. Aunt Em got up and kissed Dorothy. She gave Dorothy the lunch pail she had fixed that morning. Then she left.

Nurse Wilson put Dorothy in a little room where there was a bed and a dresser, and she told Dorothy to wait. Dorothy waited and waited, and after a while the door to her room opened and the little girl with the yellow hair came in. She was carrying a pumpkin that was carved with a pair of merry eyes and a grinning mouth.

"This is for you," said the little girl, "because soon it will be Hallowe'en." She put the pumpkin on the dresser. "Why are you here?" she asked.

"Because I talk about a place I went to once, and no one believes it's real."

The little girl nodded. Then she went away and Dorothy waited some more. After a while it began to rain.

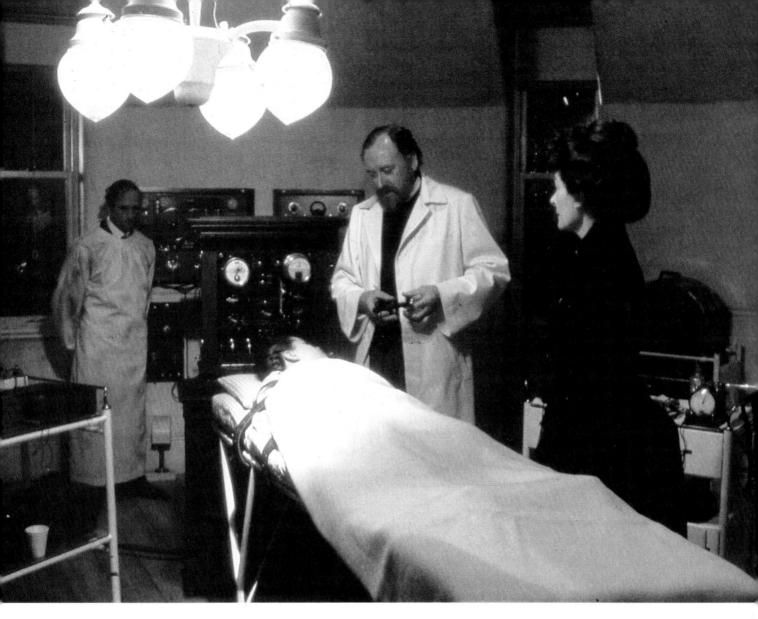

Nurse Wilson came back at last. Two men were with her. They wore white tunics and pushed a table that rolled on squeaky wheels. They made Dorothy get on the table, and they strapped her down. Then they squeaked the table down the corridor to a room where Dr. Worley waited.

The doctor was fussing with his machine. He had fastened wires to a pair of things that looked like earmuffs. When he held the earmuffs out, a spark crackled between them.

Far off in the big house, someone screamed. The men in white went out, and the nurse smiled down at Dorothy.

The doctor put the ear pieces on Dorothy's ears. He turned to the machine.

Then there was a flash of lightning. The overhead lights flickered out.

Nurse Wilson stepped away from Dorothy's side. "I'll see to that," she said. "You can check the generator."

The doctor did not answer, but Dorothy heard them both go out. She was alone with the darkness and the storm.

But then she was not alone. Someone moved beside her and the earmuffs
came off.

Lightning flashed again. Dorothy saw the little girl who had brought the
pumpkin.

"Quick!" said the little girl. "We have to get away!"

She undid the straps that held Dorothy. Then she and Dorothy fled out of
the room and down the hall. They were downstairs at the front door when
the lights came on again, and Dorothy glimpsed Nurse Wilson behind them.
Then she and the little girl were out the door and racing down the steps and
across the lawn.

They plunged into the woods that rimmed the place, and they fell, rolling and tumbling down a steep slope. Suddenly the ground dropped out from under them. Then they plunged into water—black, angry, swift-running water. Dorothy went under, then came up choking and caught at something.

It was a chicken coop that had been swept into the river. Dorothy clung to it. For a moment she saw the other girl being carried along by the flood. Then the girl vanished. Dorothy was alone, clinging to the chicken coop and riding the stream wherever it would take her.

Somehow Dorothy climbed into the chicken coop and fell asleep. When she awoke it was daylight, and she and the chicken coop were floating quietly in a pond.

Dorothy sat up. Something was making the soft "Kut-kut-kut-a-kut" noise of a chicken. It was Billina—dear, comfortable Billina—huddled in a corner of the chicken coop.

"I was trying to lay my egg," said Billina, ruffling her feathers. "I have never been so wet in my life," she complained. "How big is this pond, anyway?"

Somehow it did not seem strange for Billina to be talking. Dorothy often talked to her hen; why shouldn't Billina answer back at last?

Dorothy looked out over the water and saw that the pond where they floated was small, and that it was getting smaller every second. The water was seeping away into the ground. On one side of the pond was a forest, and on the other three sides there was sand. It stretched away for miles and miles, and it looked familiar.

Suddenly Dorothy knew where she was. She had seen that stretch of sand before. She was not in Kansas. She was in Oz! The sand was the Deadly Desert. It was a terrible place where people were turned to dust if they put even one foot to the ground.

The last of the pond seeped away. The chicken coop was high and dry on a little sandhill.

"How nice!" said Billina. "I'll scratch around and see if I can find some breakfast."

"No!" Dorothy picked the hen up and held her close. "If you touch the sand, it will be the end of you."

Holding Billina tightly, she stepped from the chicken coop to a stone that stuck up from the sand. Then she hopped to a second stone, and then to safe ground on a little mound of earth at the edge of the forest.

"Now we can look for breakfast," said Dorothy. "Then we'll go to the Emerald City and see the Scarecrow."

Breakfast was no problem. Some of the trees in the forest had lunch pails growing on them, and Dorothy picked a lunch pail as easily as she would have picked an apple. The ham sandwich inside the pail was very tasty, and there was an apple to go with it, and a piece of sponge cake.

After Dorothy and Billina had eaten, Dorothy picked a second lunch pail in case they got hungry on their journey. Then she and Billina started for the Emerald City. Dorothy wondered what they would find when they got there.

They found a ruin.

The beautiful towers were bare and gray. The splendid walls were crumbling. There were no jewels anywhere, and dust swirled in the streets. The place was ugly and desolate and dead.

Dorothy did see some people, but those people did not move or speak. They were hard and cold as statues, for they had been turned to stone. Near the city gate a circle of stone maidens held hands in frozen dance positions. These maidens had no heads.

"I don't like it here," complained Billina.

Dorothy did not like it either, but she could not leave until she found the Scarecrow. She went around a corner, and there was the Tin Woodman. He was tin no longer. He had been turned to stone like everyone else. The Cowardly Lion was nearby, his stone mouth open in a silent roar.

"But where is the Scarecrow?" said Dorothy.

At that, a terrible screech filled the street.

Dorothy whirled around and saw a creature coming toward her. It went on all fours like an animal, but it did not walk. It rolled. Instead of hands and feet it had wheels at the ends of its arms and legs. The wheels were making the screeching noise. The creature badly needed oiling.

"Chicken!" cried the creature. "Chicken! Chicken!"

Suddenly there were dozens of creatures screaming through the ruins.

Dorothy and Billina fled. Down the street and around a corner they went. They dodged into an alley. There they had to stop at a blank wall.

"Got you!" shrilled the Wheelers. "Got you! Got you!"

There was a door in the wall, but it was locked. Dorothy yanked at the handle. Then she thought of the key that Billina had found in the farmyard. Would it fit this door?

She took the key from her pocket and put it into the lock. She turned the key and the lock clicked. The door opened. Dorothy and Billina ran through, and Dorothy slammed the door.

The Wheelers screamed with rage.

Dorothy crouched to look through the keyhole. She found herself staring into the eye of a Wheeler

"Why are you so angry?" said Dorothy. "We haven't done anything to you."

"You stole a lunch pail," scolded the Wheeler. "That's forbidden, unless you have our permission. And you have a chicken with you! The Nome King doesn't allow chickens anywhere in Oz!"

"The Nome King?" said Dorothy. "Who is he?"

"He rules Oz!" said the Wheeler.

"But the Scarecrow…" began Dorothy.

"Gone!" cried the Wheelers. "Gone! Gone!"

They danced and laughed in the alley, and then they rolled away. Only two stayed behind to guard the door.

Dorothy trembled and backed away from the door. Then she turned and saw a copper man. He sat in a corner, and he looked as lifeless as everything else in that dead city. Fastened to the front of this metal person was a plate proclaiming that this was the Royal Army of Oz.

"Is he the whole army," said Billina, "or just one of the soldiers?"

Dorothy looked at the back of the copper man. She found a second metal plate with an inscription.

"'For thinking,'" read Dorothy, "'wind Number 1 under left arm. For speaking, wind Number 2 under right arm. For walking and action, wind Number 3 in the back. Guaranteed to work perfectly for a thousand years.'"

"Do you believe that?" asked Billina.

"This is Oz," said Dorothy. "It could be true."

She wound the key under the copper man's left arm.

The copper man began to tick.

"He's thinking," said Dorothy. "I'll wind up his speech, so he can tell us what he's thinking about."

She wound the key under the right arm.

The copper man ticked on for a second, then said, "Good morning, little girl. Good morning, Mrs. Hen. My name is Tik Tok, and I am the Royal Army of Oz."

"The whole army?" said Billina.

"Yes," said Tik Tok.

"What happened to the Emerald City?" asked Dorothy. "The jewels are gone and the people are all stone."

Tik Tok did not know. "Everything was fine when I was put in here," he said. "His Majesty the Scarecrow told me to wait for further orders. Then he went out and locked the door. When he did not come back I ran down, and I remember nothing after that."

"We must find the Scarecrow," said Dorothy as she wound the copper man's action. "Somewhere, somehow, he must still be alive."

When Dorothy finished winding, Tik Tok saluted. Then he took the lunch pail that Dorothy had picked from the tree. He charged out into the alley and began to flail at the Wheelers with the pail.

The Wheelers fled, but their leader was left struggling in Tik Tok's grasp.

"What happened to the Emerald City?" said Tik Tok. He shook the Wheeler. "Where is the Scarecrow?"

"The Nome King conquered the city," said the Wheeler. "He turned everyone to stone, and he stole the emeralds. I don't know what happened to the Scarecrow. Only Princess Mombi knows that."

"Mombi?" said Dorothy. "Who is Princess Mombi?"

"A witch!" said the Wheeler. "She helped the Nome King conquer Oz, so he made her a princess and he gave her the Emerald City."

The Wheeler pointed to the palace where Mombi lived. It was a huge building that had once glittered with jewels. Now it was gray and dreary.

Tik Tok released the Wheeler, and it rolled away as fast as it could go.

Tik Tok knocked on the door of Mombi's palace. When no one answered, he turned the handle and went inside. Dorothy followed, and Billina came after. The hen kept close to Dorothy's ankles.

Though the palace was ugly on the outside, inside it was beautiful—and filled with music. In an inner room someone was playing a mandolin.

Tik Tok, Dorothy, and Billina followed the tinkling, plinking sound until they came to a chamber that had mirrors from ceiling to floor. A lady sat in the center of this shimmering, reflecting place. She played the mandolin, and as she played she watched herself in the mirrors.

"Pardon me," said Dorothy politely. "Are you Princess Mombi?"

The lady did not answer, but she stopped playing. She held out a hand to Dorothy. "Help me to rise," she said.

Dorothy did as she was told. Then she and Tik Tok and Billina walked with the lady through a door in the mirrored wall. Beyond the door was a sleeping chamber with a beautiful crystal bed. Dorothy saw cabinets around the walls—thirty-one cabinets, and each had a number on it.

One cabinet was empty. One was closed. In each of the others there was a head—the head of a pretty girl. The heads were as lifeless as the plaster heads in a hat shop. Just the same, Dorothy felt sure that once they had been alive. She recalled the stone maidens dancing headless near the city gate, and she shivered.

The lady—she had to be Princess Mombi—removed the head she was wearing and put it in the empty cabinet. Then she took the head from cabinet Number 17 and put it on her own neck. Instantly it was alive.

It was a lovely head, with black hair and a pearly complexion. "What do you think?" said Mombi to Dorothy.

"It's... it's very beautiful," said Dorothy.

Mombi nodded. "Very well. And who are you?"

"I'm Dorothy Gale from Kansas, and this is Tik Tok. The hen is Billina."

"Come nearer, Dorothy Gale," said Princess Mombi.

Dorothy obeyed. "If you please," she said, "where is the Scarecrow?"

"He is a prisoner in the mountain domain of the Nome King," said the Princess. "You know, you have a certain prettiness. I believe I'll take your head. I'll give you Number 26 for it."

Dorothy pulled back, but the Princess seized her by the wrist and began to drag her toward the mirrored room.

Tik Tok charged, brandishing the lunch pail. At the entrance to the mirrored room he stopped, however. "My action!" he cried. "I've run down!"

The Princess laughed. It was a horrid sound.

"You let her go!" squawked brave little Billina. She flew at the Princess.

"You scrawny crow! I'll fry you for breakfast!"shrieked the Princess. She held Dorothy with one hand and seized Billina with the other.

"Now will you exchange heads?" she asked Dorothy.

"No!" cried Dorothy.

"Then you'll stay in the tower until you change your mind!" said the Princess.

She opened a door in the wall and dragged Dorothy and Billina up a flight of stairs. They were thrust into a dim, dusty room, and the door slammed on them. A wooden beam dropped into place to secure the door from the outside. Then Mombi clattered away.

There was a window at the end of the tower room. Dorothy looked out and saw the Emerald City. The forest lay beyond it, and beyond that was the Deadly Desert. Far, far in the distance, a mountain loomed up. It was the domain of the Nome King. The Scarecrow was there.

"Mom?" said someone in the tower.

Dorothy jumped, and Billina scuttled to hide.

"Mom?" It was a tall, very skinny creature who spoke, a creature with a round pumpkin head and dry, brittle stick arms. Someone had thrown him against the wall and left him in a heap with all his joints unhinged.

"I'm not your mom," said Dorothy. "I'm Dorothy Gale from Kansas. And, tell me, who are you?"

"I'm Jack—Jack Pumpkinhead. If you please, will you check my head for signs of spoiling?"

Dorothy and Billina examined the pumpkinhead all over. "No brown spots," Dorothy said.

"Oh, thank you," said Jack. "Now could you please put me back together?"

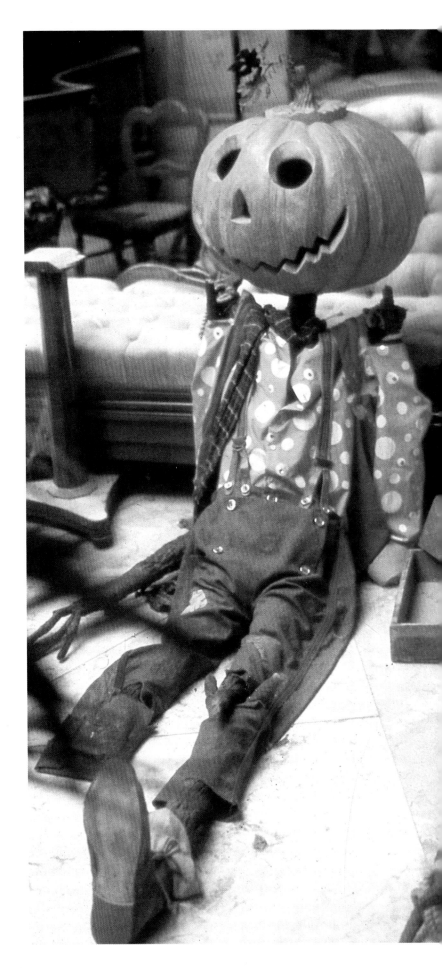

Dorothy began to sort out Jack's limbs while he told his story.

"My mother looks a lot like you," he said. "One day she made me and put me in a place where Mombi would be sure to see me. Perhaps she hoped that Mombi would be so frightened that she'd run off and never come back. It didn't work out that way. Mombi got angry.

"At first Mombi was going to pull me apart. I wasn't alive then, you understand. But then Mombi decided she'd test some Powder of Life. She sprinkled me with the powder, and it worked. Here I am!"

Dorothy had finished her work. Jack was all in one piece. He stood up and took a few stiff steps.

"Powder of Life?" said Dorothy.

"You sprinkle it on an object, and that object comes to life," said Jack.

Dorothy looked thoughtful. "Does Mombi have more of the powder?"

"If she does, it's downstairs in the first cabinet."

Dorothy's mind raced. She said, "Listen! I have a plan!"

Quickly she told Pumpkinhead her idea. It was risky, but no riskier than just waiting. They set to work.

Jack slipped his arm between the bars on the door. He lifted the beam holding the door shut. Then he and Dorothy crept down the tower stairs to the mirrored room.

Tik Tok was there. He stood motionless. Dorothy wound him, then told him her plan. He saluted and he and Jack disappeared up the stairs.

Dorothy crept into Mombi's sleeping chamber.

Mombi lay in the crystal bed. Dorothy stole past the bed to the cabinets.

The small doors were all locked.

Dorothy looked back at Mombi. She had turned over, and one hand was outside the covers. A ruby key was fastened to her wrist by a black ribbon.

Holding her breath, Dorothy went to the bed and bent to take the key. She moved it slowly, slowly down over the hand.

The witch moaned in her sleep. But the ruby key was off now. Dorothy backed away, then turned and went to the first cabinet. The key slid into the lock. Dorothy turned it and the door opened.

Inside there was a head, an ugly thing with hair like snakes. It slept.

Strange objects lay behind the head. These were Mombi's charms and spells. "Powder of Life," read a label on a tin.

Dorothy reached for the magic powder, and suddenly the sleeping head woke! The eyes opened and glared. The head twisted. Teeth snapped.

Dorothy pulled back, the tin of powder in her hand.

"Dorothy!" wailed the head. "Dorothy Gale!"

Behind their doors, the other heads took up the cry.

Dorothy slammed the door and locked it. She snatched the key and ran.

Mombi was awake and groping blindly in front of her. She could not follow Dorothy, for she had gone to bed without any head at all.

The wailing followed Dorothy up the tower stairs.

Billina, Tik Tok, and Jack were working on a strange contraption. It had
the head of a Gump—an animal that looked much like a camel, except that
it had horns and was green. This Gump had been hunted down long ago,
and the head had been put up over the fireplace. Now it was tied to a sofa.

"Do you have the Powder of Life?" asked Jack.

Of course Dorothy did, so Tik Tok fastened a second sofa to the first. Jack
tied palm leaves onto the sofas for wings, and he fastened a broomstick to
the back of the thing to steady it.

Glass shattered downstairs. The headless Mombi had smashed her way
into a cabinet. Frantic, Dorothy sprinkled the Gump with the magic powder.

Nothing happened.

"There must be some magic words," prompted Jack.

"Read the directions on the box," squawked Billina.

Dorothy did. The words on the box made no sense, but she read them
anyway. "Weaugh!" she said. "Teaugh! Peaugh!"

The Gump's glass eyes moved.

"That's it!" cried Jack. "It's working!"

They leaped onto the sofa as footsteps pounded up the stairs. Dorothy held Billina tight.

The tower door burst open, and there was Mombi—a hideous, evil-looking Mombi with snaggleteeth and serpent hair.

"So!" she shrieked. "Escaping, are you?"

The Gump beat his palm-frond wings and a hurricane of dust billowed up and filled the tower. For an instant Mombi was overcome. She staggered back and fell.

The Gump lifted into the air. He flew unsteadily out the window. The witch was left to rage alone.

Night had come. They had passed the forest and the Deadly Desert, and now the mountain loomed close. They were almost there.

Suddenly the Gump slipped sideways and lurched downward.

Then Jack Pumpkinhead's head fell off. "Help!" cried the head.

The Gump dove, and soon they caught up with Jack's head. They fell beside it for a moment.

"Look out!" shouted the Gump.

The sofas came completely apart. The brave band of rescuers fell, arms flailing and wings fluttering.

One sofa landed right side up on a mountain ledge. Dorothy plumped down on it, safe and unhurt. Billina fluttered to her side.

Jack's body fell into the snow. His head came next, and it landed on his pointed neck—upside down. Tik Tok plunged headfirst into a drift. The Gump's head thudded down.

The Nome King looked out of the mountain. He saw Dorothy put Jack's pumpkinhead on his shoulders right side up. Then he saw Dorothy fasten the Gump's head to the sofa that had landed on the ledge.

When Dorothy was finished, the Nome King spoke. "Who are you?" he said. "Why have you come to my kingdom?"

Dorothy jumped. They all jumped.

The Nome King's face was part of the mountain. Its mouth smiled a deadly, welcoming smile.

Dorothy stepped forward. "I am Dorothy Gale, and these are my friends Tik Tok and Jack. The Gump is the one with the sofa. Billina is...is..."

She stopped. Billina was not to be seen. She had gotten into Jack's pumpkinhead. She hid there, looking out through the eyeholes. The careful hen remembered that the Nome King did not approve of chickens.

"Why are you here?" said the Nome King.

Dorothy told the King very politely that she hoped he would restore the Emerald City and release the Scarecrow.

The Nome King laughed so heartily that he split the ledge where Dorothy and her friends were standing. They were sucked inside the mountain. They fell in darkness until they found themselves swept along on a river of jewels.

The Nome King's voice boomed in the cavern. "All the metal in the world is mine. All the jewels are mine." He was lying. He had stolen the emeralds from the Emerald City.

Dorothy was whirled over a great emerald waterfall. She tumbled down in a shower of gems, and she landed on something soft.

Dorothy struggled to her feet. She saw someone scrambling to get up, and she knew that her search was over.

"Scarecrow!" she cried.

"Dorothy!" The straw arms hugged her—and thunder cracked. Then suddenly the cave was dark, and Scarecrow was gone.

The light came on again.

"That is a lesson for anyone who wants to steal from me," said the Nome King, who had become more human. "I have turned the Scarecrow into an ornament for my palace."

Tik Tok, Jack, and the Gump came spinning into the cavern. Billina came too, hidden in Jack's pumpkinhead.

"All is not lost, Dorothy," said the Nome King. "If you don't mind a little risk, we will play a game. You will go one by one to inspect my ornament collection. Each of you will have three chances to guess which ornament is the Scarecrow. If you touch the right object while saying the word 'Oz,' the Scarecrow will be restored to life, and I will let him go free."

"We must try it," whispered Tik Tok, "or he'll turn us to stone."

"All right," said Dorothy.

"Then let the sofa go first," said the Nome King.

Two Nomes appeared in the wall. They pulled the rocks aside. The Gump went through the opening and the rocks closed on him.

The cave grew dim. There was a crack of thunder and a flash of light, and then darkness. The Gump had been turned into an ornament.

"But…but you didn't tell us you would turn us into ornaments if we guessed wrong!" cried Dorothy.

"You didn't ask," said the Nome King. "All right, Pumpkinhead. You're next!"

Jack, with Billina in his pumpkinhead, was soon sadly changed.

The lights came on.

"Next!" said the Nome King, and Tik Tok walked away.

A little later, one of the Nomes appeared and whispered to the King.

"Your mechanical friend has stopped guessing," said the King. "He is just standing perfectly still."

"His action must have run down," said Dorothy. "He needs to be wound."

"I see," said the Nome King. "Well, you can go in and wind him. Then stay and guess for yourself."

The Nomes opened the wall for Dorothy. She went through the hole.

She was in a huge marble chamber. Shelves everywhere were crowded with gold and silver and crystal and porcelain ornaments.

Dorothy hurried to Tik Tok. His clockwork was wound tightly.

"Don't say anything!" whispered Tik Tok. "I had to get you in here away from the King. Pretend to wind me. I have an idea that may save us."

Dorothy began to make winding motions.

"I have one guess left," said Tik Tok. "Watch me when I guess. If I'm wrong, you'll see what the Nome King changes me into, and that may give you a clue. It may help you to guess how he changed the Scarecrow."

He put his hand on a vase. "Oz!" he said.

The thunder crashed and the lightning flashed. Tik Tok was gone!

Dorothy looked all around her, hunting for something that might be Tik Tok. She could see nothing different.

Now she had to guess. She touched an alabaster bowl. "Oz," she said.

Nothing happened. She had guessed wrong, and her first chance was gone.

She guessed again, and again nothing happened.

She decided to leave the last guess to chance. She closed her eyes and put her hand out. She felt something prickly.

She opened her eyes again. She was touching a pin-cushion, and it was green. "Oz!" said Dorothy.

There was the Scarecrow, his eyes round with delight!

Quickly Dorothy and the Scarecrow began searching through the jumble of objects. "You were green," said Dorothy. "Perhaps people from Oz turn into green ornaments."

"Like this?" said the Scarecrow. He held up a green inkwell.

Dorothy touched it. "Oz!" said she.

There stood the Gump, sofa and all!

"That's it! Quick!" cried Dorothy. "Look for green things!"

Mombi the witch screeched and moaned. Minutes before she had burst into the cave. The King quickly shut her in a cage because she had let Dorothy escape. Now Mombi rattled the bars.

Scarecrow and Dorothy were still racing about the ornament room, searching for green things. The search did not last long, however. The room suddenly filled with a rumbling sound, and ornaments began to tumble from the shelves. The Nome King's great head appeared through the floor.

The Scarecrow snatched up a green porcelain fruit basket just before it hit the floor. "Oz!" he cried.

Jack appeared, safe and sound.

"Stop that!" shouted the Nome King. He had Mombi's cage in his fist, and he shook it angrily. "I'm tired of your games, and I'm tired of you!"

His hard eyes fell on Mombi. "Oh, please!" she begged.

The Nome King opened his great mouth and tilted back his head. He stuffed Mombi's cage down his throat.

Mombi screamed as she vanished into the smoky heart of the mountain.

The Nome King picked Jack up. He was going to swallow Jack, too.

From inside the pumpkinhead came a sound that froze the king. "Kut-kut-kut-kawaaaak!" cried Billina.

The Nome King made a strangled noise. Then, before he could move, the top of Jack's head came off. It fell, green stem and all, into the King's mouth. And then an egg dropped out of Jack's head into the Nome King's mouth.

"An egg!" cried a Nome. "Poison!"

The Nome King moaned and set Jack down on the floor. Billina stepped out of the pumpkinhead, angry and insulted. "Poison indeed!" said she.

Thunder crashed. The cave became pitch dark. When the light returned, the Nome King was king no longer. He was just a heap of broken stones. A pair of ruby slippers sparkled in the rubble.

Now the ground was shaking. Dorothy pulled off her shoes and put on the slippers. Pieces of the ceiling were crashing down as she clicked her heels.

"I wish that all of us from Oz may return to the Emerald City," she said.

Smoke gushed from the mountain. Then the air cleared.

Dorothy, the Scarecrow, Jack, Billina, and the Gump were on a grassy hillside. Below they could see the ruins of the Emerald City.

There was a whistling, shrieking sound, and Mombi appeared in her cage. Dorothy's wish had brought her back.

Dorothy clicked her heels and commanded that all the emeralds be returned to the Emerald City. The city below suddenly shimmered.

She commanded that the Tin Woodman and the Cowardly Lion and all the others who had been turned to stone be restored to life. The Emerald City began to buzz and hum with activity.

A volcano rumbled far off. It was the Nome King's mountain exploding. "We never found Tik Tok," said the Scarecrow.

Then the Gump turned his head. There was something hanging on his antlers—a medal made of copper. It was green with age.

"It must have fallen on you," said Dorothy. She took the medal. Then, hardly daring to hope, she said, "Oz!"

Tik Tok appeared, saluting and ticking happily. They were together at last!

Dorothy and all her friends were part of the parade in the Emerald City. Even Mombi was in the parade. The wheelers pulled her cage.

The marchers reached the palace and went into the mirrored hall. The Scarecrow took his place on the throne.

Suddenly the Scarecrow did not want to be king. "Dorothy, you stay here in Oz and rule over us," he said.

Everyone cheered, but Dorothy shook her head. "I must go home," she said. "Aunt Em and Uncle Henry will be worrying about me."

Dorothy saw sad faces around her, and she felt sad herself. "I wish I could be in both places at once," she said.

She was wearing the ruby slippers, and the moment her wish was spoken, something moved in one of the mirrors.

Dorothy stared. There was a girl in the mirror—a girl who looked like Dorothy. She wore a beautiful silken robe, and she came toward the surface of the mirror, and suddenly Dorothy knew who it was.

"It's you!" she said. "I was afraid you had drowned!"

The girl in the mirror smiled. "Help me step through the glass," said she.

Dorothy put out her hands. Her fingers touched the girl's fingers and the glass rippled like water. The image came out and the two girls stood together.

"Mom!" cried Jack, and he fainted with a great clatter of dry sticks.

"That is Ozma!" cried a voice from the back of the room. "She is Queen and rightful ruler of Oz!"

"Ozma's father was King of Oz before the Wizard came," said Mombi from her cage. He gave me his daughter!"

"And you made her a slave!" scolded Dorothy.

Ozma smiled. "I forgive you, Mombi," she said. "You've lost your magic powers, and that's punishment enough for a witch."

Ozma then went to the throne. Dorothy took off the ruby slippers and put them on Ozma's feet. "Now, if you please," said Dorothy, "would you wish me back to Kansas?"

Ozma did it, but not before she promised to look in on Dorothy from time to time. "And if you want to visit Oz," said Ozma, "I will make it so."

Dorothy said farewell to her beloved friends. It was very hard to leave them. Soon a mist rose and she was whirled away.

It was Toto the dog who found Dorothy sleeping beside Cottonwood Creek. He barked and lapped at her face, and Uncle Henry came running. So did the other men who had spent the night tramping through the fields, searching. Then Aunt Em bustled up to hug Dorothy and wrap her in a blanket. She carried Dorothy away from the creek and set her high on the seat of the wagon.

Dorothy looked across the fields and saw what was left of Dr. Worley's clinic. It was just a heap of charred timbers.

"Lightning hit it," said Aunt Em. "Nobody was hurt except Dr. Worley. He went back to save his machine."

A police van came along, and the officer in the van asked if there was any sign of "the other one."

Dorothy knew the officer was talking about the little girl with yellow hair, so she said nothing. She knew the little girl would not come back, except for the times when she looked in on Dorothy.

Aunt Em and Uncle Henry took Dorothy home then, and things were the same as they had always been.

Of course Billina had vanished from the barnyard, and no one knew what had become of her. No one, that is, except for Dorothy, who knew Billina lived happily in Oz.

Sometimes, as the days and years passed, Dorothy looked into her mirror and saw Ozma looking back at her. Dorothy never told about seeing Ozma in the mirror. If she told, Aunt Em might worry. Besides, Dorothy didn't have to talk about it. She had been to Oz, and everything there was all right!